Joycelyn & William Wilson and TJ Gordon.
For all of our descendants and legacy.
—T. t. S.

Black people past, present, and future:
this is for ALL of you.
—L. L.

SIMON & SCHUSTER BOOKS FOR YOUNG READERS
An imprint of Simon & Schuster Children's Publishing Division
1230 Avenue of the Americas, New York, New York 10020
Text © 2017 by Theresa Wilson
Illustrations © 2023 by London Ladd
Originally self-published as a poem in *Mass Matter Magic* in 2017.
Book design by Alicia Mikles © 2023 by Simon & Schuster, Inc.
All rights reserved, including the right of reproduction in whole or in part in any form.
SIMON & SCHUSTER BOOKS FOR YOUNG READERS and related marks are trademarks of Simon & Schuster, Inc.
For information about special discounts for bulk purchases, please contact Simon & Schuster Special Sales at 1-866-506-1949 or business@simonandschuster.com.
The Simon & Schuster Speakers Bureau can bring authors to your live event. For more information or to book an event, contact the Simon & Schuster Speakers Bureau
at 1-866-248-3049 or visit our website at www.simonspeakers.com.
The text for this book was set in Gilroy.
The illustrations for this book were rendered in mixed-media collage.
Manufactured in China
0922 SCP
First Edition
10 9 8 7 6 5 4 3 2 1
CIP data for this book is available from the Library of Congress.
ISBN 9781665900348
ISBN 9781665900355 (ebook)

You So Black

By
**Theresa tha
S.O.N.G.B.I.R.D.**

Illustrated by
London Ladd

A DENENE MILLNER BOOK
Simon & Schuster Books for Young Readers
New York London Toronto Sydney New Delhi

You

So

Black!

You so Black, when you smile, the stars come out.
You so Black, when you're born,

the god come out.

Black as **night** . . .

Black when it's wrong . . .
Black when it's **right**.

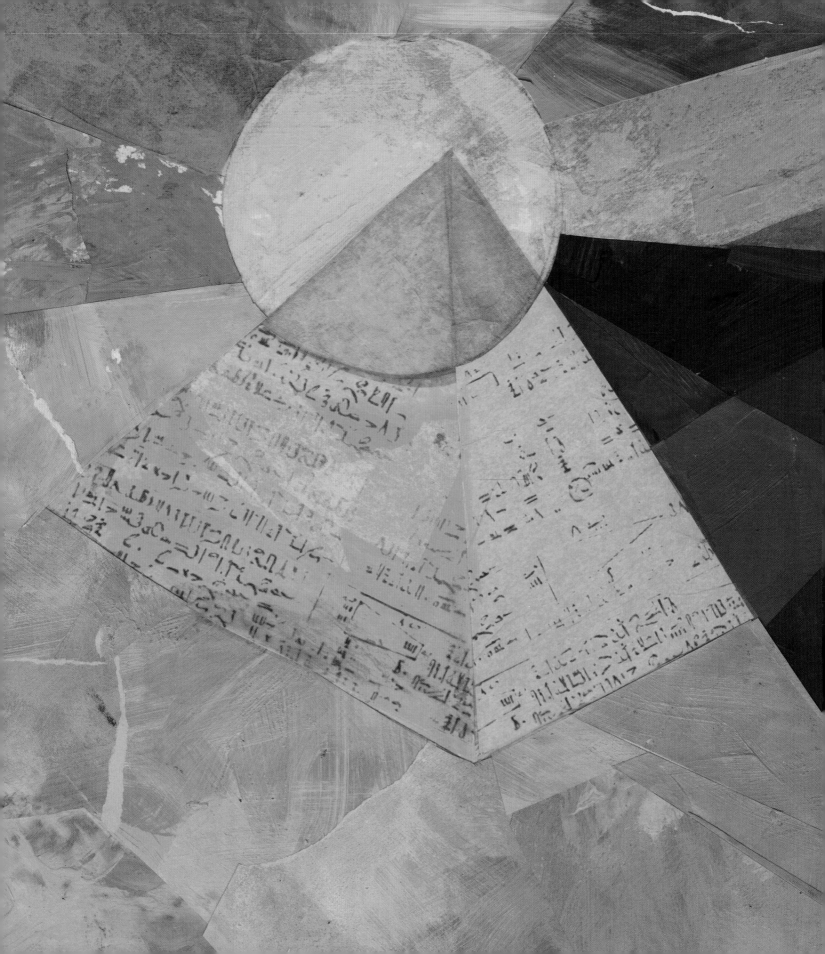

Black is pyramids and mathematics.
Black is melanized and magic.

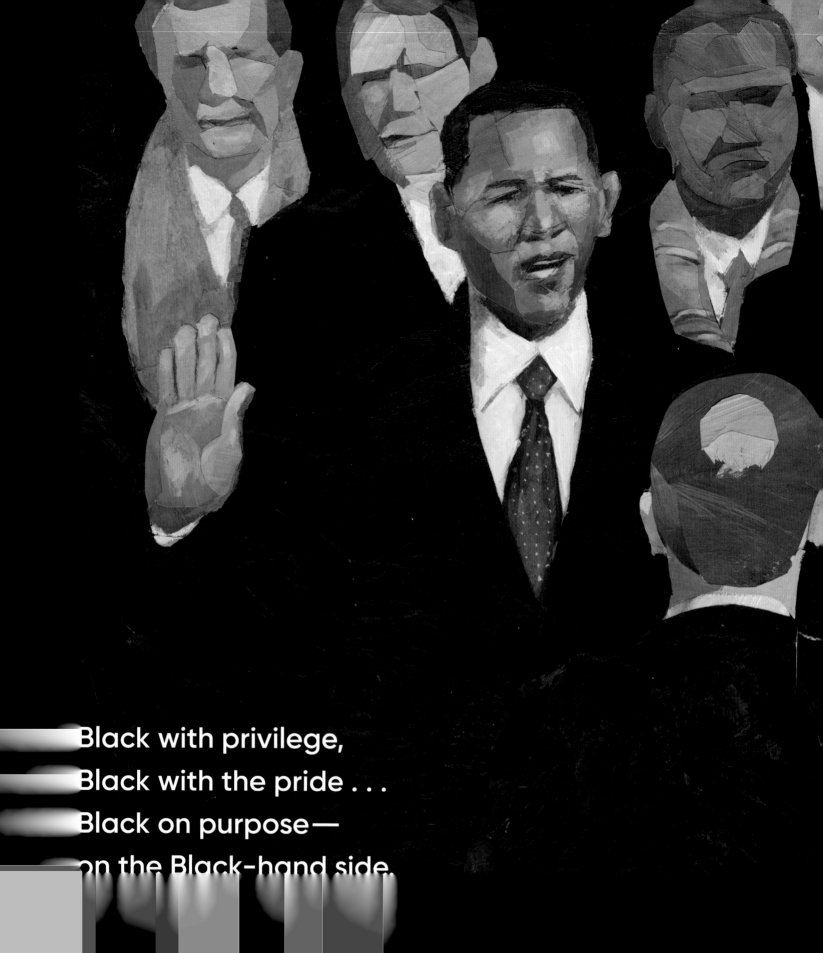

Black with privilege,

Black with the pride . . .

Black on purpose—

on the Black-hand side.

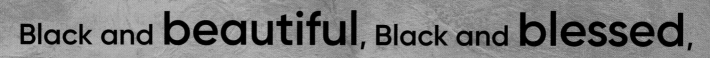

Black and **beautiful**, Black and **blessed**,

Black and so much more, Black and **nothing less.**

Black is **brilliant.**

Black is **strong**.

OUT OF THE MOUNTAIN OF DESPAIR,

A STONE OF HOPE

Black is resilient.

Black is song.

Black is **infinite**,

like **hip-hop**

or **space**.

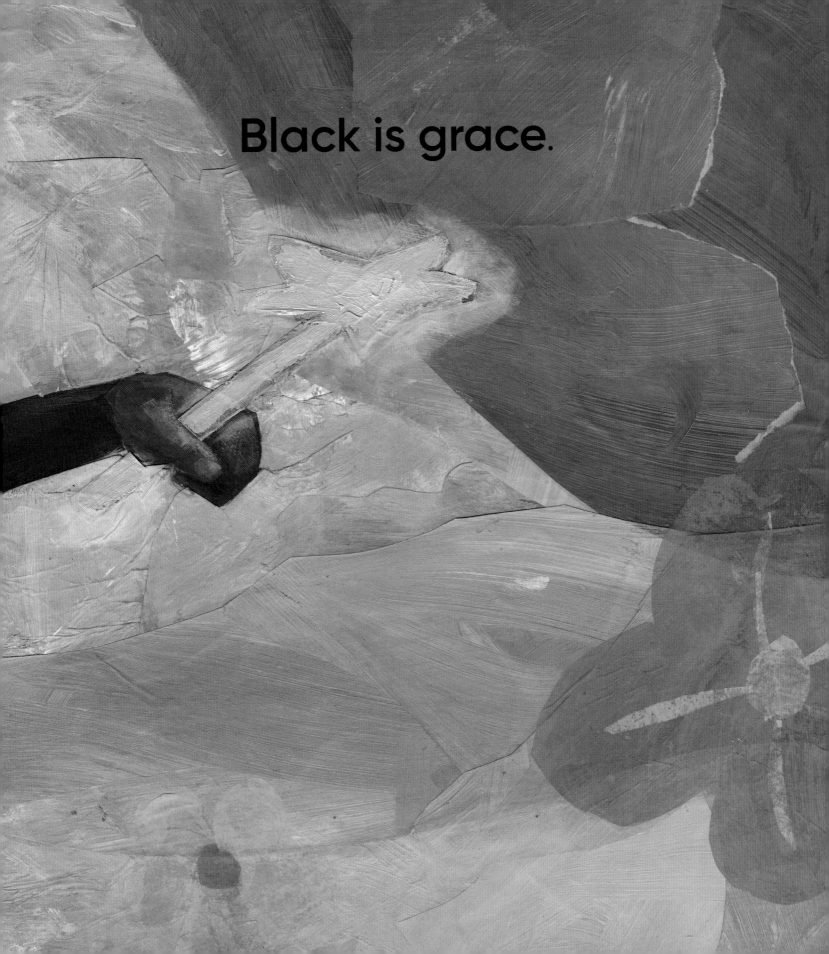

Black is grace.

Black is love.

Black makes babies—
Black babies grow **up**.

Black is hard to do!

Black is me.

Black is you.

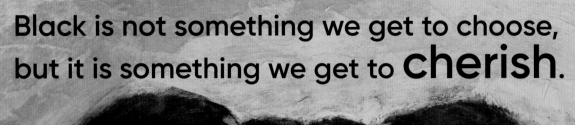

Black is not something we get to choose, but it is something we get to cherish.

It's something we get to wear with honor.
I'm Black like my granddaddy and my
great-great-great grandmama.

Black is "Lift Every Voice and Sing."

Black is letting your freedom ring and resound.

Black is

adjective,

adverb,

color,

and noun.

Black is crown.
Black is clean.

So, to the Black as all **everlasting** ...
to the Black and passing ...
and to every shade of **Black** in between. . . .

You
So
Black!

You so Black, when you smile,
the stars come out . . .
You so Black, when you're born,

the God comes out.